# About the author

Born in the South-East of England, 42-year-old, mother of six, Cordelia Fonte is a former English teacher with a passion for reading.

# The Worst Hangover

# Cordelia Fonte

## The Worst Hangover

Vanguard Press

VANGUARD PAPERBACK

© Copyright 2018
**Cordelia Fonte**

The right of Cordelia Fonte to be identified as author of
this work has been asserted by her in accordance with the
Copyright, Designs and Patents Act 1988.

A CIP catalogue record for this title is
available from the British Library.

ISBN 978 1 784654 10 8

*Vanguard Press is an imprint of*
*Pegasus Elliot MacKenzie Publishers Ltd.*
www.pegasuspublishers.com

First Published in 2018

**Vanguard Press**
**Sheraton House Castle Park**
**Cambridge England**
Printed & Bound in Great Britain

# Dedication

For my loving husband,

My children

And

My ever-supportive family.

# Preface

It's 8.03am on the first morning of the school summer holidays and the kids are still in bed. The swimming lessons are great on a Tuesday after school but they really take it out of them. I've already downloaded an audio timetables book for Cadence to use during the holidays to ensure she doesn't fall behind. It's amazing how one school can say she's meeting her targets and another be concerned that she will struggle in September as she is very weak. Don't get me wrong, I loved her previous school for the support and kindness that they gave in the really rough times but I never realised how much the sheer number of students in a class, or even the year group, could affect the level of education. Cadence is having to complete a diary for the holidays too. "Focus on the content of the sentences. I'm not too worried about spelling or handwriting. Cadence has so much to say but can't form the sentences to write it down," said her teacher. "I have given Cadence a diary to fill in. She loves to draw but please get her to write." So today we are going to take Lena to work then head in to town to find a nice A4 size book to work in. Seriously, you should have seen the pathetic attempt that was sent home. Four pieces of A4 plain paper folded in half and stapled along one edge. Firstly, that will not see Cadence to the end of the week and secondly, just because we're not particularly looking at presentation doesn't mean we can just write on any old scrap to hand in for September. Think of how proud Cadence will be when she presents a beautiful, sentence and picture filled journal of the summer to her new teacher. Of course, Alexander will need one too, which is fine as he has a treasure bag that he can fill for his first day in Reception. You wouldn't believe how ready he is for this move to 'big boy school'. He really, really hated the pre-school. Nothing to do with the staff or what they were doing but, just by my own observations, I could see it was a step back from his previous nursery. He also struggled with being with the younger children too. With Alex being too advanced and Cadence playing catch-up, things have been a bit crazy for us, without the pressure endured by the ludicrous court case. I have had an awkward, emotional, challenging, scary, heart wrenching, embarrassing, painful and confused eighteen months but with the amazing support from those closest to me.

Now I guess is the best time to rewind to the beginning and fill you in on all the details.

\*\*\*\*\*

Undoing the numerous tiny plastic bands, I had paraded in my neatly plaited fringe for the last twenty-four hours I took a long look at the roundness of my puffy face in the full-length mirror. My eyes followed the thick contours down the increased sag of too many heavy dinners and left-over incubation fat to reveal possibly the most accurate of fancy dress costumes I have ever cobbled together. Always convinced that I was more masculine in features, I opted for a male-inspired costume for Maxine's eighties' themed birthday party. The outfit was a combination of black leggings that were on the brink of being translucent under the strain, a plain white shirt, borrowed from my father as all mine would have burst open through taught buttoning, and my trusty white DMs. The only item I had purchased to complete the ensemble was the hat. A black bowler with long braids of multi-coloured nylon and satin ribbons creating shocks of colour amongst the matted frizz that was my untamed lion mane. My face was daubed with shades never before used from the eye make-up pallet, or since come to think of it. To finish the look was a money belt, fastened on the last hole, to save carrying a bag with me all night. Before you all assume that I am lacking in confidence and self-esteem, I should explain that my discomfort about my appearance is largely due to the fact that this party occurred two months after the birth of Alex in which I had ballooned to a size where I no longer recognised myself. However, it was also the first time, since giving birth, that I had been able to drink and have a laugh with my friends, passing responsibility to my husband for the evening and being able to relax.

Armed with a bottle of wine and a cheap, apple flavoured bottle of shots, I headed to the meeting house for the all-important pre-pub drinks. With everyone in the same boat, juggling young families and running homes, we opted for "Let's drink as much as we can before we head out" in order to save money. There were about fifteen of us and everyone had made an effort, though I couldn't help feeling a little smug knowing that, in comparison, my costume was by far the best. The reaction as I walked in had confirmed that. The place was filled with the usual suspects and the mood was light with mindless chat and the quick wit of the resident comedy duo, brothers Chris and Ed. Chris was Maxine's long-term boyfriend and father to her children. Ed, his younger more outrageous, banter fuelled partner in crime, had had a similar idea to me and dressed transgender for the occasion by taking off the iconic Freddie Mercury wearing false boobs which spent the night being fondled by men and women alike.

The drinks flowed and mini competitions involving shots took place until all that filled the kitchen were empties, our cue to move on. What a sight we must have been trundling along the pavements next to the main road en route to our next destination. Many of the group were in couples and walked together, the guys taking the mick out of the almost immediate complaints about sore feet and painful shoes from respective wives and girlfriends. Dressing like a man does have its benefits sometimes. The first pub was so busy you couldn't move from one end of the bar to the other without getting too up close and personal with a complete stranger. A place chosen by the birthday girl to showcase her warbling skills on an ageing Karaoke system. Thankfully it was short lived and we headed on to somewhere new, a bigger venue and a regular disco. By this time, I had consumed way more alcohol than intended and was aware of my outrageous dance moves but I didn't care, I was with the people who I'd shared some of the best and worst life experiences and nobody was judging me. Most of them knew I was a secret smoker so when I slipped out the back to the car park for a crafty cigarette no one batted an eyelid. Chris was already out there for the exact same reason. Although he had been in my life for the past nine years, I had never taken the time to have a lengthy conversation with him and tonight he looked particularly fed up and I wasn't uncomfortable with questioning his mood. It seems he had no reservations about discussing his woes with me either. It was in these few minutes that I realised that he and I were one and the same. We shared the same frustrations within our current relationships, feeling completely taken advantage of and suffering in silence. We discovered each other's ambitions and ideals and just like that I saw Chris in a completely new light, regretting not seeing it sooner and, maybe due to foolish intoxication, I said, "You know what, Chris, it should have been you and me."

# Chapter 1

"Hungover?"

The simple message that was about to change many lives forever.

I knew from the immediate response that I was forced to make the decision to end my marriage that very morning and face the fallout head on or beg and plead to struggle through the pending difficulties to maintain what was already a desperately strained relationship. Stomach in knots, I stood at the bottom of the stairs and asked Stuart if we could talk in private. The angelic faces of Cadence and Alex didn't register any tension and they continued to tuck in to their breakfast. Sitting on the edge of the bed, I bit the bullet.

"I need to tell you something and it's not very nice. You will be upset and angry with me but I can't keep this from you."

"What?" Stuart asked, chin tilted high with an almost cocky air. Already his stance had changed, his shoulders broad as he puffed out his chest casting an imposing figure towering over me.

"I saw Chris in the club last night when I was out with Megan and we were both quite drunk and I kissed him. I'm so sorry. I hadn't intended for this to happen. I'm sorry."

Touch paper lit, the reaction was as I had feared. Within seconds the door was impacting so hard with its frame that it immediately sprung back open at almost the speed that it was slammed shut in the first place. This triggered an obtuse reaction in itself and the door took the full force of a thirteen-stone recoiled fist. I knew that this could easily become very nasty and dangerous for me, yet I was not at all surprised. You see, this was not the first time I'd been witness to the rage that Stuart succumbed to following any disagreement or him not getting his own way.

The late afternoon of the christening of Cadence some three years previous had been the first time. Stuart had been drinking all afternoon at the party held at the local pub for the proceedings' celebrations and I had been left to greet guests and organise food and cakes and pictures, ensuring all were attended to, including Cadence herself. By the time we got home, I was tired and hurt that he had even suggested that he stay on with his friends to continue their session whilst I went back to our flat with Cadence, laden with food storage containers, decorations and gifts. Needless to say, I voiced my opinions as soon as we got home. Our first real row and he became a mad man. Cadence was awake and began to cry in fear as he hurled torrents of verbal abuse at me. I soothed Cadence in my arms and took her to our bedroom to avoid any further distress for her. Stuart burst into the room and yanked Cadence from my arms.

"Don't think you're having her!" A fine spray projected from his mouth as his temper took hold.

Cadence was in such a state, her face red as she screamed, hot tears rolling down her face. I pleaded with Stuart to give her back as I was just calming her down. Turning on his heel, he headed for the front door. I followed, fearing for Cadence.

"What's stopping me from leaving with her right now?" he barked.

"You're drunk and she's so scared. Look at her. Look at what you are doing to her. Give her to me." With that I took her from his arms. I must have touched a nerve as he didn't resist. I retreated to the bedroom and held Cadence close and reassured her with soothing tones, "Everything is alright sweetheart. Mummy's got you now." No sooner had the words left my lips than I heard the loudest thud. He lost it. I winced and curled Cadence tighter into my body as the sound of things being broken or damaged filled the flat. I grabbed the television remote and put on Disney Jr, increasing the volume to drown out the noise. Resting my face to plant gentle kisses on Cadence's soft dark hair I sobbed, willing it to be over. Suddenly all was quiet. Followed swiftly by the sound of keys and the front door slamming. I propped Cadence up with some pillows in the middle of the bed and went to the window. There he sat in the driver's seat of the car in silence, engine silent and with a face like thunder. I approached the bedroom door unsure whether or not I wanted to open it. With my hand resting on the door handle, I glanced over my shoulder to see Cadence with heavy eyelids, gently stroking her nose with the satin edging of her comfort blanket. I stepped into the hallway to be confronted by a head height jagged hole in the lounge door and a metal child safety gate twisted and bowed along one side, hanging awkwardly on its fixing brackets. Paperwork and toys strewn across the lounge floor were pretty much the extent of it.

Here I found myself again cowering in a bedroom asking Stuart to calm down and, subconsciously, calculating the expense of possible repairs for potential damage in this room.

"Why?" he bellowed, his face just inches from my own.

"I've been unhappy for a long time. I can't talk to you anymore."

"Is it any wonder when you're too busy running around having affairs with other men!"

"It wasn't an affair! We had one kiss. That is all." And it was, mostly. You see a few weeks previously I had been out on a girls' night and as time clocked by many of the group disbanded from the pub until only a few of us were left. Chris had also been out that night and turned up at the same place. Maxine was so drunk that she could barely sit straight at the bar. Her shirt tied round her waist sporting a large wet stain where she had vomited on herself earlier and made a feeble attempt to wash it out in the ladies' hand basin. I told Chris that what Maxine really needed was a taxi home and her bed. Chris smiled in agreement, finished his pint and helped Maxine to the door. He was swiftly followed by the other remaining group member. I assumed she was just checking Maxine was okay but to my surprise Chris returned about ten minutes later. No Maxine or our friend. It turned out that the friend had just decided to walk home and Maxine was put in a taxi by Chris and he opted to spend the rest of the evening drinking with me. I was grateful he had returned as I felt slightly abandoned by the friend. Surely its common courtesy to let someone know if you intend to go home, instead of leaving them at the bar alone. Not just that I had been fending off the advances from a rather drunk rough looking guy who was trying to get me to go back to his flat. That most certainly would not have happened. He was becoming a pain though so I turned to Chris and mouthed two simple words "Help me!" He laughed and put his arm around my shoulders protectively, pulled me closer with a firm squeeze.

We talked and joked, so involved with each other's company that everyone else in the pub faded into the background. I leaned forward and kissed Chris softly on the lips. As I moved away I thought that this is where I find out that for the past two years that the feelings I have for Chris are not going to be reciprocated. So, I looked into his eyes and said, "Shall we try that again?"

Not waiting for a reply, I kissed him again but this time his response was everything I had hoped for. Every inch of me became alive. His gentle lips pressed firmly against mine, slightly parted to allow our first intimate caress. Suddenly we were very aware of standing at the bar in a pub full of people, many of whom knew Chris and Maxine. We finished our drinks and made our escape. Hand in hand we walked home like giggling teenagers. I attempted to scale a four-foot wall but with very little elegance. Engrossed in conversation we soon noticed we were almost at my house. Chris stopped me and pulled me close to him.

"I love you and have done for some time now."

He kissed me passionately. I had no words. We continued to walk holding hands until a final corner to turn would reveal my front door.

"This isn't fair. You're going back to him and I'm going back to Maxine. It's not what I want."

"I know but we need to think about this. There's children involved. The consequences could be catastrophic. We need more time."

I don't remember feeling guilty about that kiss and right now I felt the same. Stuart's eyes were puffy and red. I hadn't noticed he was crying.

"I want you to leave. Go to your parents or something. I don't care, just leave."

He left the bedroom and headed downstairs. I followed him worried that he would involve the children. By the time I got to the bottom of the stairs he had their shoes and coats, pushing them towards the back door. They were still in their pyjamas and Cadence was starting to panic. He stood between myself and my children as he ushered them out. Cadence calling for me the whole time. Before I knew it they were in the car and accelerating down the alley. I had no idea where he was going or what he was going to do. I called his parents and told them everything. They managed to get hold of him and reassured me that the children were fine. Told me he would call me later but we needed to calm down. With that nobody would answer their phones anymore. I packed a few things in a bag and called my parents. That's when the tears came. The hurt as I realised he had taken my children from me. Not knowing where or when I would see them again. Not able to speak to them. What must they be thinking? One minute they were enjoying a lovingly prepared cooked breakfast with mummy and daddy and the next they are taken from their home with no explanation. My parents collected me and I cried the entire journey to their house.

# Chapter 2

The next ten days were a bit of a blur. Inside I was broken but outwardly I was the hard-faced cow everyone always perceived me to be. Taking this stance had worked with Stuart. We had arranged contact with the children, money and issues surrounding the car and the unimportant things. We had agreed that the children would stay with him for the short term as I was going in to hospital soon and I would need at least six weeks to recover. Being so far away from the children's school and not being able to drive would prove problematic in maintaining as much of the regular routine as possible for them. Work had been brilliant. They supported my need to take time to seek legal advice and even changed my HR files due to the request from Stuart to not use his surname any longer.

There was one thing no one had counted on however and that was Maxine. Who would have thought that the girl who was too lazy to walk her children to school, sometimes even get them dressed, who avoided housework at all costs, who would slob around her house in her dressing gown smoking, drinking coffee and getting lost in pathetic childlike animations on a social networking game site actually had some fire in her enormous belly. I had been aware from the Sunday morning that the news hit that I was the subject of an internet hate campaign started by Maxine and there had been numerous threats of violence towards me from people I had never even met. The same people that probably wouldn't know who they were looking for anyway but had jumped on the 'wronged women must show solidarity' bandwagon. Some who did know me had even upgraded my social status before slagging me off, "She's supposed to be an upstanding member of the community!" I quite liked that. It makes me sound like the town mayor or something. But in all seriousness, I was concerned for a while about being jumped in the streets by strangers who had filled the site with their ego boosting bullshit. At one point, Maxine had asked her family members to drive past my parents, Chris's parents and Megan's houses with a note of our car registrations to find out where we were. Keeping tabs on our every move and scrutinising the mobile phone bill to see how often Chris and I were contacting each other. Maxine, however was borderline psychotic in her attempts to get at me. She had, at some point, taken the time to tear pictures, of us together from previous years, in half and placed them neatly on the bonnet of my car in the staff car park. I mean, seriously, who does that? Was I bothered? Of course not. It just reinforced the level of maturity I had already witnessed from her over the years. The girl was still obviously stuck in the school playground which would explain the enjoyment she got from watching people shouting at each other on ridiculous daytime TV programmes about who did what with who and who's the daddy. The rest of us had grown up and lived in the real world. Due to the nature of my job, management told me that I needed to contact the police as she had been trespassing and it was a major safeguarding issue. So, I found myself that evening in a police station pouring my heart out to two kind officers in a formal statement against her. This was to be the first of many incidents involving Maxine and her inability to deal with the situation.

Chris and I had been in contact with each other and met up on a few occasions. He had moved back in with his parents and was adamant that he was not going back to Maxine. I was nervous of sitting with Chris's parents for the first time since the split, as a huge wave of guilt and responsibility washed over me. I had ruined the home of their grandchildren, taken their security from under their feet, the one true carer in their household and their interactive mentor keeping them on track with life and wellbeing.

"How are you, Rebecca?" was the first thing Eric, Chris's dad, asked.

"Suffering the worst hangover in history!"

"Nah, I remember waking up on a park bench once. No idea how I got there." A ripple of hushed laughter passed around the room and the tension eased. I had known these people for a long time yet I was so unsure of how they would react.

"Coffee?" Victoria, Chris's mum, was the kind of person who was no nonsense and I'm sure she would have said something if she hadn't approved of me being there. We had had many a conversation about how she disliked Maxine in the past, she sure as hell wouldn't defend her in this but she must have felt angry at the separation on the grandchildren's behalf. In her shoes, I would have been angry too, but the logical head tells me that in life these things happen and you deal with it and move on. Of course, the conversation that afternoon surrounded the recent events and they were disgusted at Maxine and her family's behaviour, yet in line with their expectations of them. I would say they were a little shocked at the sudden motivation from Maxine. The best line coming from Victoria, "Well, I never knew she had it in her!" With more stories and laughter shared at Maxine and co.'s expense it was time to head back to my parents. Chris offered to walk with me.

"I've spoken to Lena and she's cool with it. She was a bit upset about finding out on the internet but I can't change that."

"Most people, including my family, found out that way. It's not great but as you say there's nothing we can do now."

"She did say one thing though."

"What was that?"

"That she was glad it was you." Followed by a large grin. "Maxine never really did much for her anyway. She wasn't really very close to Maxine. I don't think you need to worry."

The rest of the walk was in silence. There was so much I wanted to say although now was not the time. I think Chris was still hurting and didn't feel he could open up about that just yet, not to me anyway. This would get a lot harder for all of us before things settled properly and right now I had other things to consider too.

"I want to come and see you in hospital."

"No, don't worry about that. You stay here and concentrate on your children."

"I want to. How are you getting there?"

"Mum is taking me. I have to be there for seven am so she has time to drop me off and be back in time for work. Stuart wants to be the contact for when I come out of surgery and he said he will relay the message to my parents. I'll ask them to let you know how it went if you like."

"Yeah, that would be good but I still want to see you." He grabbed my hand and pulled me close, embracing me warmly. "I care about you and I'm allowed to worry. How about I come to see you the day after the operation?"
"Okay."

*****

"I'm sorry, Ms. Hadley, but we have had to rearrange the theatre list for this morning and instead of a nine am slot we've moved you to 12.30pm. Would you mind waiting in this private waiting area?"

A rhetorical question. What would they have done if I had said no, demanded my nine am op slot back and kicked up a fuss? Probably cancelled it altogether and sent me on my way. I guess I'll just wait then. Here's a question... why do they put the oldest, most boring magazines out in a waiting room? Do I really want to be looking at whether or not I can afford to have a plush new kitchen or bathroom suite installed in my home, pokey to say the least in comparison to the grand manor on display in the pictures, when potentially I'm going to be unemployed for the next six to eight weeks with minimal benefit income to keep my head above water? Also, exactly how many tweed jackets does one need to possess before one is considered a 'Toff' among the elite? Does Lady 'Whatshername' actually tend to her own forty-five-acre garden? I couldn't care less. Today is a big day for me and the outcome could be huge. After discovering a small tumour early on in the year the need to have a hysterectomy had stepped up a gear. Prior to that I had been fobbed off for years with "Oh you are just unfortunate" or "This is normal following the birth of children". That may be for some but those that shout loud enough, metaphorically speaking, will eventually be heard. I couldn't spend the next twenty-five plus years taking changes of clothes with me, wherever I went, just in case I haemorrhaged. Periods had been the bain of my life for many, many years and now, at last the iron fist doctor was on my side and pushing to help me get some answers. It turned out that the tumour removed by keyhole surgery was benign, which was a relief and I thought the end of the troubles. New meds and the like to help prevent the development of cists which were mutating to form tumours and I wouldn't have to suffer anymore. Oh, how wrong could I be? The bleeds were increasingly more painful and frequent and I was on the verge of losing my job due to the amount of time I needed off. I contacted the surgeon who had performed my previous operation and she had given me an emergency consultation. I don't know what I had expected really, a chat and maybe a small examination. I was used to having uncomfortable situations involving women peering into the areas deemed 'NO GO!' and I had quite categorically concluded that I would have no interest in obscure sexual acts involving fists ever in the future. This examination however was on a whole new scale.

"We need to remove the haemorrhage, Ms. Hadley. Please try to relax and let your knees fall open."

Oh my God! Yelling and crying through the pain of having something extracted from my body I made up my mind that enough was enough. When it was over I requested to be put on the list to have a hysterectomy. An internal camera had also shown two new tumours developing and so it was agreed. It had been the longest four month wait but now I was here and not backing out or creating a reason to not have this done. Stuart and I had discussed the implications at length and as I had been sterilised after giving birth to Alex, decided that the best option was preventative surgery. Nobody likes to talk about "The Big C" but if you have the opportunity to stop it I don't think there are many questions to ask.

"Ms. Hadley. We are ready for you now."

I don't think I have ever felt so alone.

# Chapter 3

"Oh dear. If I ever get to that stage, when I'm old, where, as my soup spoon comes up my tongue comes out to meet it then it may well be time to call it a day!"

"What?"

"Over there," Chris pointed out an elderly couple, in the hospital café, a few tables away. I laughed but it hurt. It was good to be out of my ward room although it looked like I would have stay yet another night. The wound wasn't draining and the nurses advised that until it does I was staying put. Chris had come to visit as promised and it was good to get a little light relief following my earlier visitor. Stuart had turned up. He struggled to make the normal genuinely concerned chat until he couldn't suppress his true intentions for the hour round trip. Question after question about what had happened and what I felt for him, for Chris and the future for us both. No mention of the children. I understood that he was hurting but I was not in a position to get into that type of discussion having been out of surgery about ten hours. I wouldn't give him any answers and asked if we could meet to talk this over once I was home. This was a trigger for another tirade of verbal abuse and, in the end, I asked him to leave. Stuart was clearly using my vulnerability to intimidate me and so I pressed the call button on my bed. My room light flashing and the buzzer ringing out in the corridor was enough to force Stuart to leave. He almost collided with the nurse as he hurried out the door. The nurse lent over me to silence the buzzer.

"What can I do for you, love?"

I couldn't tell her anything but I was so tired from the operation and my heart heavy with guilt I couldn't hold it together any longer. A huge wave of emotion took over and I cried once more. Though not for myself. I missed my children desperately and had absolutely no control over what they were experiencing, what they were being told and how they were being cared for. The nurse's soothing tone and reassurance only fed the hatred I was feeling for myself. I didn't deserve her kindness even if she was doing her job. She poured me a fresh cup of water and stood next to my bed until I had calmed down a bit.

"How's the pain?"

"Being upset isn't helping but it's okay." Truth be told, I wanted it to hurt. A sort of punishment I guess.

Chris had been a welcome distraction and the snail's paced walk, with him as my crutch, was just what was needed. Reluctant to leave at the end of visiting time he planted a gentle kiss on my forehead.

"I wish I was taking you home this evening."

"I know. I'll call you tomorrow."

In actual fact if he had held on for a few more minutes he would have been able to take me home. No sooner had he left the nurse came in and checked the drain. Apparently, the walk had been just the thing to kick start the draining of the wound and I was good to go. The only thing now was I would have to wait to be collected by my mother.

Back at my parents' house that evening I had managed a civilised conversation with Stuart and he agreed to bring the children to see me the following morning. I spoke to them both and they were tearful, missing me. Cadence had sounded quite wheezy and so I told Stuart to get her checked out at the doctors first thing in the morning and bring them to me after.

When the children arrived next morning, Alex ran towards me with open arms but Cadence was quiet and withdrawn. She looked a ghostly shade and once inside she just curled up into my lap and closed her eyes. Stuart said she had had a rough night with her coughing and asthma and that she had an appointment to see the practice nurse later that morning. The time went by all too quickly and I placed a tearful Cadence in the back of the car.

"Let me know what the doctor says."

"Will do."

Not half an hour had passed when I received the call that would throw me. The assumption that Cadence needed a prescription for salbutamol and steroids wasn't going to cut it this time.

"We're in an ambulance on our way to A&E. Suspected pneumonia," Stuart said.

"What? What are they going to do? Where's Alex?"

"He's with my parents. I'll keep you informed."

"But I can't get to the hospital. I have no car and I'm not supposed to drive. I'll call my mum and I'll be there as soon as I can."

Cadence looked so small, so thin, so very unwell. Oxygen mask covering her pale lips. Her cheeks drawn in, enhancing every laboured intake of breath. Loud beeping from the heart monitor was distressing yet comforting at the same time. The monitor was so sensitive that alarms would sound at the slightest movement. I held her close, as tight as I could. Her eyes welling with tears. I couldn't show her that I too just wanted to sit there holding her, sobbing, scared by the seriousness of her illness. That's how we sat until the nurses came around to take her obs and give more medication. There was no change and so now we had to play the waiting game, hoping the antibiotics would do the trick. Cadence was so brave. Not a murmur of complaint when prodded and poked for the IV drip being pressed sharply through her fragile skin. Not one single tear as blood was taken and in the morning more tests to determine the best course of action for her fluid filled lungs.

"Mummy will be back tomorrow, sweetheart. Daddy is going to stay here with you at the hospital. I love you so much my precious little girl," I told her, placing gentle kisses on her forehead. Cadence was tired and I had Alex to think about.

"Call your parents, Stuart. I'm collecting Alex on my way home. He's staying with me."

# Chapter 4

Four days of tests and strong antibiotics saw Cadence right as rain. She has to be one of the bravest and strongest little people I have ever met. Now it was time for some R&R at home with her brother and enjoy the build up to Christmas. Both children would be with Stuart over the Christmas holidays but it goes without saying that both children would rather have been with me and more so now that Cadence had been poorly. They needed their mummy. Only the love and reassurance that a mother can give when everything is wrong and scary and not as it should be in the perception of a two- and five-year-old. My initial protests fell on deaf ears and the children went with Stuart from the hospital straight to his future girlfriend's house. This caused yet more tension as, although fully aware of the seriousness of Cadence's condition, Maxine insisted that she would not go outside to smoke. I cannot begin to explain how livid I was that a girl who claimed to be a good mother would not put a child's health before her own selfish need for cigarettes. Maybe it was the fact that it was my child that needed the attention and yet, at the same time, I'm not convinced she would be any more considerate for any of her own children. For years they had been dragged up in a filthy house and as toddlers they would have nappies so full that they would hang low between their knees, running riot behind the closed sitting room door. Once, before the separation, I had visited and one of the twins had defecated in their nappy and, as it had been left for so long and become so full, the weight had caused it to come undone. The youngster, not knowing any different, then proceeded to take handfuls of faeces and smear it across the iPad and into the carpet and soft furnishings. Maxine's solution was to use a few baby wipes on everything, including the child's hands and then close the door on them yet again, returning to her coffee, cigarettes and laptop games.

Questions had been raised about the slow development of one of the twins. Although you could take into account that he was premature, he wasn't yet able to utter a recognisable word. The most obvious reason for this would be that he had no interaction with anyone other than his sister during the course of the day. As a firm believer in you get out what you put in to your children's upbringing, it stands as a fair example that no or little interaction will be detrimental to the basics and natural progression. It was also completely obvious that the sister was favourite amongst family members on Maxine's side. The constant neglect of being shut away in the sitting room led to numerous visits to A&E for the poor little lad. Anything ranging from nasty knocks to the head to sliced open hands on a glass. He would never complain though and would always greet me with the warmest, cheeky grin and huge hug. Both children would relish in the attention if I was babysitting for them, climbing all over me to be as close to the story books as possible, joining in with actions and animal noises, laughing at my character voices. They loved the characters being brought to life. Of course, more than anything, they just loved the fact that someone wanted to be there with them.

Christmas Day saw the children not wanting to leave me. Stuart and the children had joined my parents and me for dinner and spent a couple of hours with us. There was obvious tension but we remained civil in order for the kids to have the Christmas they were expecting and most certainly deserved. Cadence was so much better and Alex had been helping to look after her, watching her like a hawk. He was so cute in telling everyone that his sister was poorly and he was making sure she took her medicine; fetching and carrying her inhalers and spacer and the medicine spoon from the kitchen drawer. Every now and again he would ask Cadence if she was ok, especially following a coughing fit. Although he was the usual boisterous two-year-old, he had a heart of gold. Clearly older than his years in his outlook on things, yet completely innocent and unaware all at the same time.

The heart wrenching goodbyes were cut short by hurried shuffles to the car by large brutish hands and promises that I would see them the following evening.

"You can use my car when you are able to drive, Bex. I'll add you to my insurance whenever you are ready." My eldest brother. We'd never been close as kids or teenagers. In fact, we positively hated each other at times. Threatening to seriously harm one another frequently but, as adults and maturity would have it, all that passed and with us having children within months of each other we were now on common ground and supportive when needs be. We never lived that far from each other, and at one point only a road away, but visits were few and far between. Though I always knew that he would be there if I needed him and he never let me down.

"Can I use it tomorrow, please?"

# Chapter 5

I'd been there about ten minutes. I hadn't even taken my coat off. The kids had shown me a few of their presents but had just wanted to sit with me and cuddle on the sofa. That's when the all too familiar tone crept back into his voice. He knew when to start. No other witnesses but the children. Today was the suppressed anger from Christmas Day. He needed to vent, yet the disgusting language that he was using just helped to confirm the reasons I shouldn't be with him. His complete disregard for the children made me feel sick. I sat there as he towered over me, shouting obscenities. Cadence curling in closer, tighter under my arm. Her warm tears began to fall on to my supporting forearm. Alex had moved away to the other end of the sofa but his eyes never left his father. I had not raised my voice at all in my attempts to calm the situation but he had become an imposing figure looming over my daughter and I.

"Daddy, stop saying things like that to Mummy," cried Cadence. Her meek voice shaking in fear.

"Do you know what your mother is? Shall I tell you? You won't want to cuddle her then. She's a dirty, cheating slut that goes around kissing other men and not your daddy. She's a fucking filthy cunt!"

"That is enough!" I stood up. Looked him straight in the eye. Now I was angry. "You do not subject my children to this emotional abuse."

"Emotional abuse!" He scoffed. "I will say and do what I want in front of MY children. They need to know what you are and how we don't need pieces of shit like you in our lives. Get out of my house, NOW!"

His rage was building. I didn't know what to do for the best. Stay and risk the impending violence or go, leaving the children with him, removing myself from the situation and allow him time to calm down. I chose the latter. I needed to get myself sorted asap and then have my children with me. Save them from this hell. Protect them but I would have to be smart. Bide your time Bex, bide your time.

The next few weeks went by really quickly. Stuart had changed tack and was trying the nice approach.

"We need to sit down and talk. You owe me that at least."

"Ok fine. We'll talk. My parents are on holiday so we can speak privately here. Come around about ten o'clock if your parents can watch the kids. Bring your diary and we can put some contact arrangements in place too."

I'd only seen Stuart briefly, since Boxing Day, on a Sunday when he collected the kids and he was not allowed over the threshold. I would often not speak to him at all. Not through being rude but afraid of the reaction and in attempt to keep things from the children.

"I need to know if there's any chance for us. You're not telling me anything. Are you with Chris now?"

"No, I'm not with Chris. I told you when it happened that this was a drunken kiss. There was no affair or anything."

"So, what went wrong? Why didn't you talk to me?"

"I haven't been able to talk to you for years. If I broach any subject that you might not like you hit the roof and start trashing things." I was the other side of the kitchen and clearly observed the slight sadistic smirk twitching in the corners of his mouth.

"That's rubbish. The only time I've done anything was when you've pissed me off."

"Oh, so it's my fault you can't control your temper, is it?"

"Well, you tell me of the occasions where it wasn't because of you."

"For a start, there was the time that you punched the side pillar on the car in temper, leaving a big dent that you can still see today. That was due to you reversing into a wall. I wasn't even in the car but Cadence was. Then there was the time that you punched the light switch in Cadence's bedroom, in front of the kids, because the kids had emptied toys all over the floor. That was witnessed by Chris and Maxine's son who had been round for tea. I had to apologise and explain to them what had happened when I dropped him off as it was the first thing he told them when he got home. I was so ashamed and I hadn't done anything! When friends have been round for dinner you have thumped your fists loudly on the stairs when the children were making too much noise or not doing as you asked, in an attempt to show your authority through intimidation. Am I wrong? All the others were when we were arguing, I admit, but not over anything serious."

"Like?"

"Like the most recent repair in the front room, where you thought I was in a mood because I had had to go to the shops for something for tea straight from work and then start cooking as soon as I got home. The house was a mess and all you had done during the course of that day was sit at your parents drinking coffee. I was tired and had nothing much to say so you started yelling and when I told you to stop because the kids were getting upset you started swearing, stomped into the front room and picked up the first thing available, being the TV remote, threw it against the wall shattering it and taking a chunk out of the plaster. Cadence was sobbing and I was comforting her in the kitchen. You came back through to the kitchen and barked "What's up with you?" at her. I told you that she was scared and do you remember what you said? You said, "She'll get over it". What a great dad that makes you".

"Right, well I don't remember that."

"You don't remember me having to buy filler and you repairing and repainting the wall?"

"Well yeah, but!" He just shrugged his shoulders.

"But what about us? We've been married for nearly ten years, together for eleven. Are you going to just throw that away on a kiss? If you say that nothing else has happened then I believe you. We can work through this. I meant my vows when I said them. Obviously for you they were just lies."

"No, that's not true. I meant them at the time but you've changed and I've changed and together it just doesn't work anymore. You don't seem to realise that since you gave up work I have struggled to keep a roof over our heads, pay for everything including your debts, which I have contacted the company and told them that I will no longer be responsible for, running the car and on top of that keeping on top of the housework etc."

"I've been doing my bit recently."

"Yes recently, when you began to suspect that I was not committed to this marriage anymore."

"Yeah, I guess. I knew something wasn't right. That's why I was starting to sit and listen to sad songs when you weren't around."

"Oh."

"Well, look at you. You look amazing. I fancy you more now than I have done for years. I want to make this work but you don't do you?"

"To be honest, the way I feel right now, no. I did love you and I still do to some extent but I think that's because you are the father of my children. I'm not in love with you."

"Do you love him?"

"I don't need to explain myself to you but as things are at the moment I'm confused about what I feel for Chris."

"So, you do?"

"As I said, I don't know but I'm sorry this is the end of our relationship."

"You know the neighbours have said to let you go and give you some space and time. They think you'll come back. So maybe that's what I'll do and we can see how we go when you realise that this is a mistake."

"We'll see."

"You know that since you've been gone I think about you a lot in the evenings when I'm alone. Ironically, I've been looking at a website that Chris told me about ages ago. Did you know he likes porn?"

"What? Do I really need to know this?"

"Well, he laughed. "You should know that I still get turned on by the thought of you."

I couldn't help but laugh too. He was being the most open about sex that I'd ever known but I did feel a little sick.

"That's enough of that. It's just a bit weird. I think you had better go. I'll call the kids tonight as normal."

# Chapter 6

"Good to see you back, Bex. How are you?"

"I'm okay thanks. Still healing and awaiting results but definitely on the mend."

Here I was again. It's like I'd never been away. Though there were a few faces amongst staff that I didn't recognise. It won't be long before they're knocking on my door though, wanting me to babysit some of their unruly students. My regulars were pleased to see me and I them. Now to get myself back into a routine but slowly. I had agreed my own phased return with my team and line manger as that's what I would have expected if it were any of them.

It didn't take long to get back into the swing of things and on my fourth day back I had an unfamiliar PA appear at my door.

"Hi, are you Rebecca?"

"Yes."

"Hi, I've been asked to drop this off to you." She handed me a letter.

"Okay. Thanks."

She didn't hang around for me to open it and, once I did, it became clear why. Luckily Harriet, my union rep, worked in the same building as me and, leaving one of my team to supervise the handful of settled workers, I headed straight to her for advice.

"Bex, that's ridiculous!"

"I know, right. As if they don't know the seriousness of the operation or something. I've kept them in the loop from the beginning til now and I haven't gone over my recovery time or anything so what's the problem?"

"Leave it with me. I'll make some calls."

I was actually lost for words. The business manager had been so supportive of me during the really rough times of my illness and now here she was requesting a meeting to discuss a possible warning due to my sick absence. She had said she understood. She herself had been through something similar but without the cancer element. Her operation hadn't been as drastic either.

As it turned out, the area manager for my union also thought this was a crazy situation and took the case on personally. A few weeks later I was there in that meeting faced with the business manager, the Head of HR, my union area manager and my on-site representative to minute it all.

"Hi, Rebecca. I'm the Head of HR. My name is Mrs. Dyer and it has been brought to my attention that we need to discuss the amount of sick absence you seem to have accumulated recently. Now, I don't want you to feel that we are ganging up on you or anything and please don't be afraid to speak to us and tells us what's really going on. As I'm sure you can appreciate, we have to keep the interest of the school at the forefront in these matters and we need to review whether or not the workload you currently have is suitable at this time and what more we can do to help support you." She was very condescending in her tone but I remained silent and the business manager picked up from there.

"Bex, how are you feeling?" The smarmy two-faced grin of insincerity sprawled across her face.

"I'm fine." A bit of a lie. I was worried sick that I was going to lose my job or, at the very least, my promotion. I wasn't about to lose face in front of her though as she would just turn that to her advantage. I said nothing more.

"We think that the amount of time you have taken recently is reflecting on the support offered to the students. We haven't been able to cover your unit. The Head refuses to pay for a substitute teacher as you're not of full teacher status. This then meant that the students had to return to mainstream classes and subsequently caused the teaching staff, in some cases, great distress."

Still I said nothing and it turns out that I didn't need to.

"I would like to take this opportunity to bring a few things to your attention if I may?" A rhetorical question from the surly gentleman with the monotone that demands your attention.

"Ms. Hadley, as you are fully aware, has had a considerably stressful time following the recent long illness complications that were diagnosed as a potential cancer and after numerous sick certificates and hospital appointments she was advised that as a precautionary measure she was to undergo an operation. This particular operation was major abdominal surgery and following this she is subjected to regular checkups every six months. It is not like Ms. Hadley has been off with coughs and colds."

This short opening statement caught the Head of HR off-guard as she threw a one raised eyebrow look to the business manager as if to say, "This isn't quite the story you have been telling us."

He continued.

"Ms. Hadley has been caused unnecessary additional worry due to these ridiculous claims that she has somehow exceeded her sickness limits. In actual fact, it transpires that, as business manager, you have shown a degree of incompetence. Ms. Hadley has only been paid for two months at full pay and the following two months at half pay. In actual fact, it clearly states on her contract that she is entitled to six months' full pay and six months' half pay as her previous employment was carried over as a continuation. Therefore, I suggest that you go back and review your figures. Ms. Hadley is due some back pay. I would also like to ask what exactly you have done to support Ms. Hadley. Was she offered any extra support on her return to work? Why hasn't Ms. Hadley had a return to work interview with an occupational therapist? May I see a copy of the agreed phased return?"

"Erm". I must admit it was good to see her squirm. Flushed in the face, she needed to explain herself, not only to my representatives but, it seemed, also to HR. Paperwork suddenly appeared and the look on her face said it all. "Yes, I see now that Ms. Hadley has continuous service and I will need to amend that accordingly. As for the return to work interview, we were unsure of when Ms. Hadley would be back."

"If you find Ms. Hadley's last sick certificate from the hospital it clearly states the last day of absence and so an appointment should have been made. Do you have the certificate there?"

More paper shuffling and there it was, dates and all. She couldn't deny it. HR were not impressed.

"As I understand it, Bex has agreed her own phased return with her team."

"That's not her place, though, is it? You, ultimately, are responsible for managing these situations and you are more than happy for this poor young woman to have to fend for herself whilst not fully fit both physically and possibly less emotionally now. I suggest these matters are cleared up quickly and, with regards to the impending formal warning, that I assume was the intention behind this meeting, I recommend that it be disregarded."

He changed his focus. "Mrs. Dyer, I would like you to email me as soon as you have recalculated the missing earnings and I expect this to be no longer than a couple of days."

"Of course. Rebecca, I can only apologise for this mix up, however, I want to make you aware that any sick leave from now will obviously be scrutinised. Please don't think that we don't understand that people become ill from time to time but it must be a genuine illness and we may need certificates from a doctor even for the smallest ailments."

"I think Ms. Hadley has taken everything you have said on board. I would like to call this meeting to a close as I don't feel there is any more that needs to be said."

I've never been hugged so tightly by Harriet.

# Chapter 7

Mostly things had settled a bit. I was still being hounded by continuous insults from Maxine and her cronies and she had been very vocal about her new sex life, with Stuart of all people. Social networks were alight with constant updates on her 'sexy man' and what they would be using in the bedroom. Information that, quite frankly, would make anyone's stomach turn, especially if you knew them.

Work was fine and I was starting to get my finances in order to look for somewhere to live. Chris and I had been on a date, around his birthday, just a few drinks in a local pub where a local band were playing. It was a good night. We never seemed to be short of something to say. Always able to finish each other's sentences. Truly on the same wavelength.

Just as edges were smoother I was tossed a curve ball. My parents were still away and I wasn't expecting them until the weekend when my phone rang. It was my dad's mobile number. Being a family of believers in 'no news is good news' my heart instantly leapt into my throat.

"Hi Bex, it's mum".

"Is everything okay?"

"We're at Heathrow. Your dad has suffered with his heart whilst we were away and has spent the last few days in hospital. Originally a suspected heart attack but he has been looked after well and we made the decision to come home early so he can rest and see the specialists."

"Oh. Is he alright?"

"He's not a hundred percent, that's why we're coming home. Don't worry though, he's better than he was."

"How are you getting home?"

"I'm driving."

"Is that wise? You've been travelling for hours. You must be exhausted. I could get someone to bring me down and I'll drive you back."

"No, don't do that. I'll be fine and, besides, we could be home in the time it takes you to get to us. I just wanted to let you know what was happening. We will see you in a few hours."

"Well, only if you're sure. Is there anything you want me to do?"

"No, it's fine."

"Okay. I'll let the boys know. Have a safe journey. Take care."

Dad recovered quite quickly and the specialists had stepped up a gear with medication and possible procedures. What didn't help was the stress created by the insurance company but all is well that ends well and a few weeks at home saw him back on his feet and back to work. Holidays abroad were put on the back burner, not that it would stop my parents getting away.

Before I knew it, I was sat in a tiny clinic waiting room. Today was results day. I had been worrying over the possible outcome for the last few weeks. The trials of being able to park anywhere near the clinic had detracted from that for a while but now, sitting and staring at the over read posters with that weird, surreal, warm and fuzzy feeling in my head that makes you want to fall asleep and uncomfortably clammy hands, I wasn't sure if I wanted to know.

"Ms. Hadley, please."

I followed the nurse through an unnecessarily complicated set of corridors. The clinic had been deceptive. I envisioned an aerial view to show a mass of intertwining pathway buildings, much like the sprawling roots of a giant oak. The nurse herself was young and quite plain. She didn't appear to be particularly confident and made no attempt to introduce herself. In fact, she hadn't said another word since the waiting room. I just hoped that she wasn't going to be the only person in the room with me.

"Good morning, Ms. Hadley, I'm Dr. Habib. Do you mind if we are joined by our trainee nurse, Sarah today?"

"No, that's fine."

"Please have a seat. I have reviewed the biopsy results and I'm pleased to say the tumour was benign so nothing sinister to worry about. How have you been?"

"Pretty good. I did have a small infection developing where the drain was removed but a course of antibiotics sorted that out."

"Okay, good. I will need to examine you anyway so I'll check the area and make sure it's clear. Now I don't know how much you were told before leaving the hospital but you are lucky to get away without the need for a colostomy bag. Your tumour had been surrounded by endometriosis cells and they had spread so far they had attached the tumour on your bowel. During the surgery, the cells were cleared and cut away as close to the bowel as possible. Have you had any trouble going to the toilet?"

"No, nothing like that." A lot of information to process. "I didn't know about that but everything seems fine."

"And have you been sexually active at all?"

"No. I was told not to be until I had attended this appointment."

"That's good. I will need to take some swabs and give you an internal examination and that may affect the results. Would you mind undressing your lower half and laying on the bed, please. Let's get this bit out of the way now."

I hated this type of examination but it was necessary and hopefully the last time. The doctor was talking through the whole thing, showing Sarah what would need to be done to complete the swabs. The pelvic floor test was the most embarrassing, not because of how intrusive it is, because of the comment that followed.

"Well, that's very good. Possibly the strongest muscles I've felt."

I didn't have an answer for that. I just smiled. Thankfully that was the end of it and I was soon dressed and back in the chair at the desk. After filling out a short questionnaire, I was given my repeat prescription and sent on my way. It wasn't until I was sat in the car that the wave of relief hit me. I had to call my mum to let her know. Hanging up from that phone call saw me succumb to the tears and it took a good five minutes to regain composure before heading home.

# Chapter 8

Things were great. I was ignoring the childish behaviour by Maxine and Stuart. Refusing to speak to him and, as far as I was concerned, she no longer existed. Chris and I had been on quite a few dates and I was feeling more loved and respected than in any of my previous relationships. It was a far cry from the, so-called, marriage farce I had endured for the last ten years. He supported me. He was so kind and caring, hardworking and dependable. I trusted him completely and fancied him like mad.

The opportunity came up for me to rent a friend's house for a year whilst he went travelling and it seemed to make sense to ask Chris to take this on with me. A test to see how well we worked together. As a team. United in the face of all the controversy.

So, here we were settled, working and enjoying time together and with the children. Fitting everyone in the effectively two-bedroom house was a bit snug but cosy and homely. Of course, we had to replace the furniture that we both had left behind and that obviously played on the jealousy from Maxine. Phoning Chris every day with something to question, complain or bitch about. The rumour mill went into overdrive once more and I was finding out more about the décor and layout of my new home than I had already planned myself. Laughable really. Apparently, we were buying a house, a new car and getting married. Well, the latter was certainly not going to happen as I was still married to Stuart. It did start to wear me down though and I was waiting for the next thing that she didn't approve of, like it was any of her business. In the end, I decided to confront her face to face. The conversation went better than expected but then she wouldn't be hostile to my face. I know that she has always seen me as quite a hard person, who wouldn't take any crap from anyone, that's why she would always hide behind me if she was in a confrontational situation. Everyone had perceived me to be that way, but the years with Stuart had seen my confidence dwindle and in the last six months I had had to regain it, slowly becoming the person I once was. We agreed to move on and stay out of each other's way. She wanted to be civil, yet I just didn't want anything to do with her. Not even speak to her. That was that. Or so I thought.

A month passed with more hassle and ridiculous arguments instigated by Maxine. I had no part in it. Though it was mostly directed at me, poor Chris had to put up with the grief. It was then that we discovered what a nasty piece of work Maxine could be.

We had spent a lovely weekend with the children, Cadence and Alex had returned to their father earlier in the day and Chris was out returning his three. Lena hadn't been over that weekend, something I was quite glad of. I had stepped outside for a cigarette when I heard a really loud thudding on the front door. I assumed it was Megan as she had previously said she would pop over for a cuppa. Megan would knock and then just walk in but she hadn't come out to find me which I thought was weird. I stepped back inside and the house was still empty. Oh well, I'm sure whoever it was would try again or leave me a message to say they'd been. Chris got back only a few minutes after and was busy listening to a voicemail on his phone. He stood in the doorway to the hall, barely in the house and the colour drained from his face.

"What's wrong?" I mouthed. He held up his hand to indicate he wanted me to wait a minute before he could answer.

"Erm, I need to speak to my dad."

"Why? Has something happened?"

"I promise I'll tell you when he gets here but I want him to come around."

Chris wouldn't say anything more. His phone kept ringing and he let it go straight to voicemail.

Soon Eric arrived and Chris huddled us on to the sofa in the front room.

"Now I need you to hear something that's been left in a voicemail on my phone. It's not very nice and I don't know what to do. Just listen and then tell me what you think."

"Is that Chris there? You better pick up the fucking phone mate 'cause mate I tell ya I'm fucking ringing one more time. You better fucking pick the phone up, cunt, do ya hear me? You owe us… We took the fucking debt from Tony Wright. Now I tell you now boy, we've been round your fucking house right, Lamon fucking Road or whatever it is, number 8. We fucking missed you loads of times. You fucking better talk to me boy! 'Cause you're in fucking trouble. I took the debt over. Four grand I want off you! Or else I'm gonna break your fucking neck. Tony Wright gave me the number right. I've got a fucking picture of you here and your fucking Mrs. Fucking Maxine Smith or whatever her fucking name is. I tell you something pal if you don't pick the fucking phone up in a minute when I ring you again, I'll fucking be round your mum's alright? And you're gonna get fucked up mate. Don't you fuck with me when I'm trying to talk to you boy! Don't you fuck with me. You fucking pick the phone up when I fucking ring!"

We sat in silence. None of us knew what to say. I had never felt so scared. Someone had been round to our house, on numerous occasions with the intention of harming Chris, over owed rent. I thought things like this only happened on TV. You don't expect it to happen to you. I had questions but looking at Chris's face now was not the time.

Chris spoke, "That's not all. He's left two more that I haven't heard yet. This is the next one."

"You better pray boy! You better fucking pray! You better ring that Tony Wright and you tell him you want to fucking pay him the fucking money, 'cause I tell you something, pal, if you pay me… Ah, man. I'm gonna break your fucking neck. I'm gonna break fucking Rebecca Hadley's fucking neck and every fucker in your family. Don't you fuck with me boy when I… I'm fucking telling you answer the phone! You fucking answer the phone to me boy! You hear me? You better fucking pray that Tony Wright will let you off because if I fucking find you mate, I'm gonna fucking rip you apart. You better answer the next time I ring, I tell you now!"

Chris gestured that he was going to play the next one. Again, no one said anything.

"I want a thousand pound this week or else we're gonna come and see your Mrs. Alright? Just get it sorted. We want one thousand pound, ya know what I mean? You pay it to Tony Wright. You hear me son or else your Rebecca girl is gonna cop it as well! You're all in'fucking'volved now, all of ya! You understand me? Your mum, every fucker! Get it paid! Get it paid quick!"

I didn't know what to say. I got up and went to the kitchen, poured myself a glass of wine and just stood there trying to take it all in. What the hell was going on? I knew Chris had some outstanding rent to pay from the house he shared with Maxine before he would be released from the tenancy agreement, but this was something else. How had I become involved? Tony Wright didn't know me and I didn't know him so how had this guy, leaving vile threats on Chris's phone, found out about me? I could hear Chris and his dad talking in the sitting room. I heard the words 'police' and 'too far'. I had been thinking that there was really only one way to deal with this and that was to go to the police.

"Are you ok?" Chris was very pale, his meek voice enhanced his sudden vulnerability. I had never seen this in him before and it was awful. He'd been so strong for me through the recent upheavals, now I had to do the same for him. Although I had been mentioned, these people weren't really after me. It was Chris that was going to bear the brunt if they managed to see anything through.

"I agree with your dad. We need to go to the police now."

"Okay. Are you going to come?"

"Of course I am. I sure as hell don't want to be here on my own. What if they come back?"

"I don't think they've actually been round. It's just a scare tactic."

"Well, there was a really loud banging on the door whilst you were dropping off the kids. I thought it was Megan and expected her to come through and find me in the garden, where I was smoking, but she never appeared. It was probably them. Thank God, I had gone out the back. If I had opened the door God knows what might have happened. Can you imagine if you had left ten minutes later? The kids would have been here still and what might they have witnessed? It doesn't bear thinking about." Tears pricked the back of my eyes and I turned away. I would not let this get to me or at least I wouldn't show that it already had.

# Chapter 9

The next few weeks saw us regularly visited by police with updates about what had been investigated. I didn't feel safe and refused to have my children stay at the house. Our weekends were spent at my parents. I couldn't tell them what was going on. I don't know why. Maybe I didn't want them to think that I'd gone from one disastrous relationship to another. I didn't feel like that but I know that's what they would think.

Some of the officers were very helpful, and one in particular had not gone unnoticed by myself or Megan. He was a young and handsome man whose approach to the situation made everyone instantly feel at ease. One of his colleagues on the other hand was very abrupt and rude and almost scoffed at the claims, that was until he heard the voicemails. Then he had to take it seriously. Chris's phone was sent off for the information to be extracted but we weren't holding our breath. The chances were that the people responsible would have ditched the phone and as they had withheld the number there was no real way of tracking the calls. Tony Wright obviously denied all knowledge, even though he was mentioned in the threats, but the police didn't pursue it any further with him.

I had broached the subject with Chris about how I had been dragged in to all of this. Told him how I now didn't feel safe in my own home and that this wasn't my argument or debt. I was convinced that the only way that Tony Wright knew I existed was because of Maxine and the giant wooden spoon that she used to stir as much crap as possible. Ultimately, I thought she was responsible for giving out our new address too.

"There's nobody else who is carrying such a vendetta against us, who has the knowledge and connections, to make this happen. I'm telling you she's behind this."

"Look, I have been with her for years. I know what she's like and she wouldn't do this. She just doesn't have it in her." If only he knew then what we were soon to discover.

Chris did ask her and of course she denied knowing anything. In my mind, this was all her and she now knew it. That only fed her hatred and jealousy and she stepped up her campaign once more. Maxine had asked for Lena to babysit for her over her birthday weekend. Lena, of course, wanted to spend time with her younger siblings and so it was arranged that she would looked after them until eleven thirty p.m. at the latest. After all, she was only a teenager and she had managed to get herself a part time job locally that required her to be up and out fairly early in the morning. Chris and I agreed that I would go out to collect her rather than rely on taxis on a Saturday evening at that time. We also set Lena a challenge of secretly dropping comments of ridicule to the unsuspecting acquaintances that would also be present when she arrived at Maxine's house. Quite possibly the funniest was for her to guffaw loudly when in the presence of 'Cletus'. Of course, Cletus wasn't the person's real name but it was fitting for his appearance and mentality. She did it too. Texting us to let us know. Oh, the simple things. The evening was soon to become a different, not so light-hearted, state of affairs. I wasn't going to collect Lena until I knew she was ready to leave, that way I wouldn't have to see or engage in conversation with Stuart. I texted her at eleven forty-five p.m.

"Are you ready?"

"No. They're not home yet. I've tried to call but there's no answer."

"Ok. I'll get your dad to call Maxine."

It seemed Maxine wanted to enforce the fact that she thought she was in control of us and initially refused to answer the phone or text messages. An hour passed and Chris was fuming. I had even contacted Stuart and told him that they were taking the piss and needed to get back to Maxine's. This fell on deaf ears. The only message that seemed to make an impression was when I said I was leaving in ten minutes to collect Lena and if they were not there I would contact the police to inform them that the children were left home alone.

I sat a little way down the road outside Maxine's house and texted Lena to let her know I was there. The street was pitch black due to the not so ingenious idea by the council to turn off the street lights at midnight. All of a sudden, my car door was thrown open and a heavily intoxicated Stuart loomed over me, aggressively.

"Why the fuck has Chris got my number?"

"Because he was trying to contact someone to tell him what was happening with his daughter. If you two hadn't been so inconsiderate we wouldn't now be in this situation." He had no argument for that.

"Well, you tell him to delete it as soon as you get back or else."

"I'm not scared of you anymore but, as usual, it's been a pleasure."

I moved to reach for the door but he had already begun to throw it closed with such force that I honestly thought the glass was going to break. In hindsight, I wish it had. I would have had him arrested. He stormed in to Maxine's house. Lena still didn't come out. I was getting concerned. Then she appeared and she was very upset. Not only had Maxine not paid her like she said she would, but as soon as Stuart had entered the house he had backed Lena towards the door and was screaming in her face to tell her father not to contact him again. Lena told me that he was like a wild man and she was really scared. A feeling I was all too familiar with. She should never have been brought into this. She was, after all, an innocent child who was doing what she thought was a favour and by no means had shown any sign of taking sides. Well, this incident surely would cement a different opinion for Lena and that bridge had well and truly been burnt.

# Chapter 10

Lena was a sweet girl. Very intelligent and mature for her age. She had taken the decision a few years before to change schools as she could see that her potential was not being fulfilled where she was. It had paid off too. Her grades had been great and she got everything required for her college course. The course, however, was quite a long, tiring slog every day. On top of that she had mounting pressure from her mum at home and was spending increasingly more time at our place.

We got on great. She had told Chris that she could confide in me and I was supportive of her more than she had ever known from Maxine and, to some extent, her own mother. Her mum was a little neurotic. Not helped by the smoking of cannabis. Things had become quite tense and Lena needed some breathing space. She had spoken to her mother many times over the years about living with her dad but the idea was quashed without further discussion. Her mother was difficult to say the least. Her ideals and expectations were fuel for disagreements and excuses to retreat to her room and sulk. During her much younger years, Lena had been put upon far more than a child ever should have been, expected to prepare babies' bottles and feed and change her younger siblings, punished for not conforming to the unrealistic image of home life that her mother fixated on. On top of her regular school work, Lena was expected to do at least an hour of extra maths or English at home each night, books purchased by her mum from the local book shop. She would even be set a certain amount of work to be completed when away on holiday with her dad and his side of the family. Of course, they didn't go in for any of that and wanted her to be a little girl, as little girls should be. Experiencing life outside of the books and developing her social skills. Chris and his parents had often told stories of how she was a nervous little thing who would shy away from people and not talk if she didn't know you well enough. Even as she got older the latter was true. I had known her for a good few years and she had only ever said a handful of words to me. Don't get me wrong, she wasn't ever rude and would always say hello but she wouldn't make conversation and her appearance would be brief.

Lena was happy and relaxed whenever she visited us and we could talk about anything, often laughing uncontrollably over something really stupid. Chris noticed our friendship growing and would grin if he walked in to the sitting room and found us huddled on the sofa watching trashy TV. Lena comfortable enough with me to throw her legs across my lap. She had been toying with the idea again lately of mentioning a move to our house permanently to her mum, but she wasn't going to get that chance. The decision was soon out of her hands. Wendy, Lena's mother, had sent Lena a message whilst in town and asked if she could stop by as she needed to talk. Lena was worried. Didn't know what to expect. I was freaked out a bit that a woman who had judged me solely on what the internet Orc and her keyboard warriors had said about me was coming to my home.

Sat around the dining table, drinking tea was the last thing Lena had expected from her mum and she obviously had something she needed to say but was skirting around it as much as possible.

"So, how are you?" A pointless question as they lived together and had only see each other the day before.

"Yeah, fine." Lena was obviously thinking the same as me.

"I've just been in to town and brought these huge pumpkins. They were so heavy to carry here. I don't know how I'm going to manage them all the way back to your grandads. What have you been up to?"

"Nothing much. Just been shopping with Bex."

"Did I tell you about the great time I had when I went home? Everyone was so happy to see me. All my friends looked after me when I was there and I realised how much I really missed them. I don't feel like that about anyone up here. No one missed me when I was away. No one tried to call me to see how I was. I had such a good time. It just felt right. People down there are different and want me around, you know. They didn't want me to come back up here. They want me to go home permanently and I may be considering it. You know that you're step-dad and I haven't been getting on so well lately and we sat down last night and had a long discussion about where we think the relationship was going. I just don't feel appreciated enough here, by him, by you or the girls and look at how well you've done. You are following your dream and I need to follow mine. There's nothing keeping me here. I know this may be difficult for you to understand but I need to go somewhere that I feel happy and I gave up my dreams years ago when I left my home."

"But this is your home!"

I got the box of tissues from the sitting room. Lena was heartbroken. Wendy talked at one hundred mph and I don't think she realised that some of the things she was saying were so hurtful.

"Not my real home. Yes, you and the girls are here but I have a plan and when I get settled you can come and join me, if you want. You've wanted to live with your dad for a long time now and so this is your chance. You seem really happy here and we've not been getting along so well lately, maybe that's a lot to do with me not wanting to be here anymore but all the same we might be better living apart for a bit."

"What about Andrew?" Andrew was Lena's step-dad and father of her younger sisters.

"As I said, we had a long talk and, although I know he loves me, we agreed that things were not as they should be and he needs to let me go. He got upset but he knows that deep down this is the right thing to do. I'm going to go back to Ildon. My friends are happy to put me up. I just have to put in for a transfer with work and then I will know when I'm going. I will be staying with your grandad until then."

"So, you've got it all worked out then?" A rhetorical question but Lena felt Wendy needed to try and answer it. "Huh?"

"Listen, this is going to be hard for everyone and I need you to look after the girls for me. I plan for Annie to come with me but Andrew isn't happy with that idea at the moment. Tanya will be better here as she is more like her dad anyway."

"You want to split the girls up?" The look of disbelief on Lena's face took Wendy aback.

"Not for long, but there will be holidays and weekends that we can all be together and, once you see my home, I know you'll love it and you will want to stay. You could even transfer your college course and do it down there. Tanya can wait until she has finished school and start a college place down there too. With Annie being so young she will make new friends and the schools are lovely in Ildon."

The conversation continued to circulate around the delights that awaited Wendy in Ildon and Lena became increasingly more upset. Not once did Wendy offer a consoling hug, just beetled on about how Lena would be fine and that she had options, never give up on herself and focus on the deeper meanings and happiness. Yep, the woman was a fruitcake and I had to bring an end to the mumbo jumbo that she was beginning to preach.

"Listen, I don't mean to be rude but we need to head out again soon. How about I give you a lift to where you are heading and give Lena some time to take this all in?" I didn't expect an answer as I was effectively throwing her out. I needed to let Lena digest this and Wendy needed to give her the space she thought was necessary for their relationship to survive. The car journey was quiet and once back home I just held Lena tight as she sobbed into my shoulder.

# Chapter 11

The police investigation seemed to have slowed and we had heard nothing more from the anonymous person who had left the voicemails. Again, we started to relax. Of course, with someone like Maxine in your life and constantly in your business, the peace was soon shattered.

This time she had made a direct attempt at costing me my career. Making false allegations about me to my work. Little did she know that I had rumbled her before it even got brought to my attention. I had seen her with one of the keyboard warriors walking away from the main building and, low and behold, that afternoon I was asked to a meeting with the acting line manager. Once I explained the situation to him and the reasoning behind her complaint we had a bloody good laugh at her expense. He told me that as soon as she had opened her mouth to speak, in the interview room, he had clocked her for what she really was, "A shit stirring nobody, with nothing better to do than try to cause trouble for others." I had to laugh. Such a well presented, highly religious man. I did not expect him to say that. I was happier now that he knew the full story and he encouraged me to go back to the police. That's exactly what I did and she was issued with yet another harassment warning. I messaged Chris to tell him to brace himself for the fallout and, as predicted, it was as pathetic as before. She tried to use Chris's children against him, once more, by preventing them from staying at the weekend. A plan she wouldn't see through but, none the less, she was guaranteed a reaction. She couldn't see that she had created this situation and was forever bleating on about how she wanted it all to stop, yet continued to antagonise everyone over any tiny little thing. She must have spent her days sitting at home planning her next attack, sifting through messages and social networks looking for something to make a big deal out of.

For the rest of us, we had better things to do. Lena had settled well and was much happier. Though her mum had tried to say that the conversation in the dining room that day had gone completely differently and that Chris had taken Lena away from her. Of course, this was far from the truth but things hadn't gone exactly as Wendy had planned and she was still hanging around.

Chris and I were great together and soon the conversations had turned to our future. Chris had bought me a lovely ring for my birthday, which had sent the gossips into a frenzy. It was not symbolic of anything at the time, but Chris had picked it up from the kitchen window ledge where I had placed it while washing up, and was now standing sheepishly in the sitting room doorway.

"What's up?" I asked.

He moved in front of me and stood there for a moment. Then, as he lowered himself on one knee, I began to blush.

"You don't know how happy you make me. We are so alike and just know each other so well. I have been in love with you for years and sometimes have to pinch myself to realise the reality of what is now our life, here, together. You are an amazing person and we've been through so much. I wouldn't have wanted it to be with anyone else. I truly believe you are my soulmate and I want to spend the rest of my life with you. Will you marry me?"

"Erm, you know I'm still married, right?"

"Well, yeah, I know but I want you to know that I'm serious about us, about you. It can be a long engagement."

"Then, yes, of course I will marry you!"

"I know it's a bit shit asking you in the sitting room with a ring that was your birthday present but we can get you a proper one later."

"I'm not bothered about the ring." I laughed. "I thought you were against marriage anyway?"

Chris stood up and collapsed into the sofa beside me. "Only against marrying Maxine!"

Lena was happy for us, as were Eric and Victoria. I don't think they ever thought they would see Chris get married as he had been so adamant about it not being for him before. I called my parents and told them and they reacted better than I thought. I expected them to question if I was rushing things and frown upon it due to me still being married to Stuart, but when I visited them a few days later they had a card for us with their congratulations. This was the only one we received as I guess many thought it wasn't going to be. We would announce it formally once my divorce was completed and then have the celebration that this news deserved. We did, however, cuddle up on the sofa and leisurely consume a couple of bottles of wine that evening.

Our focus soon changed to that of where we were going to live once my friend returned from his travels. I had recently landed myself a new job and, with both of us now working in the city, it made sense to look for something nearer to reduce commuting times. We looked at a few places but nothing really stood out as somewhere we could settle. Money was good and we were able to look for something with enough bedrooms for everyone.

# Chapter 12

Things continued as everyday life does. Work was good and there was a continuous low-level buzzing in the atmosphere created by the search for the place we could call home.

The children were enjoying their weekend visits and we enjoyed the opportunity to spoil them rotten. No one could have foreseen the day that I thought my world had ended. Of all the crap and stress we had been through nothing could have prepared us, me, for the shock and devastation I was about to endure.

The children had been over for the weekend as normal and had all had a great time. Sunday morning and the kids were tucking in to their cereals at the dining table. I was in the kitchen making a brew when Cadence called me.

"Mum, I don't like this breakfast."

"Oh. You've had it before, haven't you?"

"Yeah, but it tastes weird."

"Okay, love, what do you want instead? Some Weetabix?" Cadence nodded. I took her bowl and gave her a fresh one with two Weetabix and sugar sprinkled over the top, just the way she liked them. I returned to the kitchen. Two spoonfuls in and Cadence began to cry.

"What's wrong?" I asked.

"I can still feel the way it tastes!" Strange thing to say. I went to her and looked her over. Nothing visible and then without warning she threw up. So much vomit. Maybe she was unwell and the cereal had just upset her stomach.

"I need a wee, Mum."

"Okay, sweetheart, you go through to the bathroom and I'll sort this out. If you still feel sick you stay in there and I'll be with you in a minute."

Slightly wobbly, Cadence got down from the table and plodded through to the bathroom. The bathroom was directly in my eye line and I called to her to leave the door open so I could see her from where I was. I glanced up when I heard the toilet flush and saw Cadence struggling to remain upright whilst pulling up her pyjama bottoms. She was so pale, almost grey. She was swaying now and trying to steady herself on the edge of the bath. I dropped everything and ran straight through the kitchen reaching her just in time as she collapsed into my arms. Her skin was clammy and almost blue. I could see the veins beneath the surface of her almost translucent cheeks. Her heart was pounding so fast through her back. Muscles in spasm so tight in her jaw that she had cut her own gums with her clenched teeth. She couldn't catch a breath. Short rapid intakes as she struggled to inflate her lungs. Mucus began to pour from her nose restricting the only other way to get oxygen to her limp body.

"Call an ambulance!" Chris was standing in the doorway. I have never seen a man look so scared. He was ashen and speechless.

I laid Cadence on the floor and prized open her jaw. Her tongue had swollen, completely filling her mouth. I pressed it down to see her airway so narrowed, her plight for oxygen increasingly desperate.

"It's alright sweetheart, Mummy's here. I've got you. I know it's hard, but try to slow your breathing down and take in as much as you can."

Her eyes were bulging and bloodshot under the pressure. My little girl was dying in front of me and I felt so helpless. Three more breaths and she closed her eyes. Silence from her blue lips.

"Cadence! Cadence!" I was shouting at her, shaking her shoulders. In that instance, a switch was flicked inside me and I automatically adopted my teacher mode. It sounds strange but I suddenly became someone else. No longer distraught, panicking mother but strategic and sensible adult with the knowledge to help in these kinds of situations.

Tipping her head back, I again tried to force open her jaw. It was impossible. I couldn't hold it. So, immediately I wiped the mucus from her nose and gave her two large breaths of air, watching her chest rise as I did so. Nothing. I really didn't want to start compressions. The thought that I may break her fragile ribs in such a tiny delicate little body. How could I hurt my child like that? I decided to administer two more breaths and this time on the second one she threw up again. I have never seen anything like it. At that moment the paramedic arrived and scooped her up and rushed her straight in to the back of the waiting ambulance. I stood dazed for a second, then followed quickly.

# Chapter 13

Stood just outside the bay in A&E, I was looking at my beautiful little girl, lifeless and weak. She was so small, her tiny frame barely visible as she lay on the starched white sheet. There was a buzzing in my head and I was shaking from top to bottom. A bustle of nurses of all different coloured tunics and a tall stocky woman leaned over Cadence. I couldn't see what they were doing exactly but she was soon hooked up to many machines and a cannula had been put into her hand. A saline drip hung above her head and two, maybe three, large needles of clear fluid injected through her hand.

"I have given Cadence adrenalin to help reduce the swelling. Can you tell me what happened?"

I explained as best I could but, to be honest, I was in shock and can't recall the words that came from my mouth. It must have made sense as the doctor thanked me and went back to attending to Cadence. I think she had introduced herself too but it didn't stay with me. I was only interested in Cadence staying with me. The bathroom scenario had seen me calling to her vacant eyes "Stay with me! Please stay with me!" Over and over. A female police officer had also attended the call and was listening in on the conversation with the doctor. I hadn't noticed her standing there prior to that and I turned to her.

"Your house is on our immediate response list due to the current investigation and so I was deployed as soon as the 999 call was received. I have all the information I need. It sounds like your little girl is lucky to have a mother like you. I'll leave you now. I wish her well."

She checked her watch, made a note of the time in her flip pad and then tucked it into her breast pocket. She quietly left and my eyes caught the glare of Stuart.

"Huh! She obviously doesn't know you!"

What a complete bastard. Now is not the time to pick a petty argument. Our daughter was fighting for her life, for Christ sake!

"You can come forward now. Cadence is stable. She had an allergic reaction called anaphylaxis. The swelling is reducing slowly but she doesn't look as poorly as she did when she arrived. Well done, mum." A comforting squeeze of my left arm.

Cadence lifted her frail, skeletal hand out to me as I approached the bedside. Her scared eyes still slightly bloodshot but not a tear in sight. Stripped to the waist with heart monitor pads causing endless beeping in my right ear. A sound I would welcome for the rest of my life. Her right arm resting on a pillow. Her hand engulfed in giant white dressing and tubes connecting her to the drip.

"You gave Mummy quite a scare." I said brushing her fringe back from her clammy pale forehead. Holding her hand, I stroked her face gently with the other. Cheeks glowing and full but her lips now back to her usual fleshy pink. A nurse came forward, cup in hand. "Would you like some water, Cadence?" A nod and a sip and then her head resting back on the pillow, eyes fixed on me.

"Mummy, I'm cold." It was like the day your baby mutters their first words. The thrill and excitement fill you with the wave of pride. For me it was thankfulness. No permanent damage done to that amazing little figure who lay too far away over a cot side high on the bed. I stood on tip toe and reached for the blanket to cover her. I engulfed her with the warmest embrace, yet scared that she might break under too much pressure. It was then that my first tear fell.

The tears continued to roll silently down my cheeks and they were showing no sign of stopping. Eventually, Cadence was moved to the children's ward and was placed in her own room. Chris had contacted my parents and Stuart had contacted his. Everyone was there. My mother consoled me, "The doctor said your actions probably saved her life. You saved her life." My mother was crying now too.

It was now midday and Cadence was sat up in her bed chatting like nothing had happened. The bizarre series of events was now something for the memory bank and she seemed right as rain. Stuart said he needed to go home for a shower as he had just thrown on some clothes to rush to the hospital. I suddenly became conscious that I was standing in front of everyone in a pair of Winnie The Pooh pyjamas. Everyone agreed that the grandparents would stay with Cadence until we returned and Stuart gave me a lift home.

The journey was silent and when I walked through my front door alone, Chris's face drained of colour.

"Oh no! Has she…?"

"She's fine. She's fine." I collapsed to the floor and Chris rushed over, fell to his knees and sat with me, holding me as I sobbed.

# Chapter 14

The house had undergone an out of season spring clean. Specialist appointments had revealed that Cadence had multiple allergies, mainly with things that could be ingested but we couldn't rule out the possibility of contact and airborne triggers. So, food cupboards were emptied and all products checked and, if need be, thrown away. All the cosmetic products in the house were also checked and discarded if anything contained any of the possible trigger elements. Carpets were washed, bed linen and toys cleaned and we now adopted the longest shopping trips in history! It was worth it though. I never want any of mine or Chris's to experience anything like that again, ever.

For Cadence, life was back to normal and she was good at checking with adults whether she could have certain treats and sweets. We were armed with Epi Pens in case such a reaction occurred again but, hopefully, we would never have to use them. I would sit at every meal time watching her, looking for any sign that she wasn't well. My nerves were on edge from beginning to end of the weekends.

The other household was slightly more blasé about the whole situation and continued to keep potentially harmful products and order random takeaways in. I feared for her. To be honest, I feared for them all.

I had noticed that we were starting to accumulate more Prosecco bottles for recycling. I was eating less and drinking more. I knew what was happening. I had been here before. The slow lulling was upon my shoulders and the hatred was returning. I had been through so many emotions lately that I think the old faithful was the only one left. I took the decision to up my meds myself. No time for doctors' appointments and you'd be lucky to get one anyway. Now at the higher dose, I also continued to self-medicate with the Prosecco. I was easily making my way through three bottles a night and still driving the forty-minute journey to work every day. No one at work knew about the struggles at home and I wanted it to stay that way.

I had an appointment to meet Stuart and a mediator, advised by my newly acquired solicitor. I was sick of him and Maxine dictating to us what we can and can't do with the children and when I could see them. So, I was taking the necessary steps to get them back with me. To safety.

Sitting across the table from him I suddenly felt vulnerable and meek. I was back there, intimidated and controlled. That smirk on his face was noted by Barbara the mediator. Her pen hadn't stop scribbling notes since he arrived. She opened the discussion informing us that if we were unable to come to a suitable arrangement mutually, then she would inform my solicitor that we should take the issues to a family court. This is what I wanted as I knew damn well that Stuart was not going to give up the children. He had too much to lose. He would only get £52 a week for caring for his father and then would have to sign on the dole. He wouldn't be able to afford the upkeep of the home I had left behind. At the moment, he was enjoying having his rent and council tax paid in full, reduced utility bills, full social benefits and excessive maintenance transferred from my account each month.

"What would you like to say to Stuart, Rebecca?"

As if the room was now pitch black and I was under a spotlight in the interrogation chair, "I would like Cadence and Alexander to come back and live with me, as agreed prior to my operation." There I'd said it. Not as confidently as I'd have liked but it was out and I wanted a response.

"I don't ever remember agreeing to that. It must be another one of your lies!" he barked.

"I have concerns about their wellbeing and, in light of recent events, you need to show more consideration for the children. Your house is filthy and you continue to have and eat things that could be harmful to Cadence."

"Well, she nearly died when she was with you!"

I was stunned into silence. Barbara stepped in.

"Now, everyone here is fully aware that there is no blame for what happened with Cadence and, in fact, it is a blessing in disguise that now you are able to accommodate her needs accordingly."

Stuart's head shaking, he slumped back in his chair, arms crossed, looking like a petulant child.

"You have no idea how it feels to have your children taken from you. I'm their mother. I need them and they need me. I miss them so so much. It's painful. I can't explain it. They are not pawns to be used in whatever ridiculous game you think you are playing. If you asked them now they would say they wanted to be with me and you know it!" I was feeling stronger. The fight was coming back.

"They don't need you! You're a filthy whore!" he spat the words at me with such venom. He turned to Barbara. "Did she tell you what she did? The reason we're in this situation? What a dirty little bitch she is, running around with another man behind my back?" And it went on and on. Barbara scribbling notes, trying to calm him and direct him back to the actual point of the meeting. He just continued in his rage until Barbara called an end to it and asked Stuart to leave.

Barbara kept me in her office and asked security to ensure Stuart had driven out of the car park before she would let me leave. She told me that, as Stuart was so volatile, she would refer us to a family court without question. A burly security guard walked me to my car.

At home on my own, two thirds of a bottle in and I was sobbing in the bathroom. The soft tissue still made my eyes and nose sore through the constant wiping. A deep breath to compose myself and that's when I saw it.

I hadn't thought about it for years, and as a teenager it was almost cool to do it. Stupid really and I knew that now but I'm a failure. I'd lost everything and I needed to be a mum so desperately.

You're a disgrace, Bex. What must your parents think of you now? You've done nothing to make them proud, just drifted through life and forever needing them to bail you out financially. You're an actual fuck up! Do you know that? You've been in an abusive marriage and allowed the monster to continue to control you and endangered your children. What kind of mother does that? And just look at you! Yes, you've finally lost most of that blubber but now your skin is sagging and your hair is thinning as you lose large clumps of it on a daily basis. You're ruined. You've done this.

Finally taking my eyes away from my reflection I saw the blood running down my arm into the sink. Seven tidy, but quite deep, scores just above my right elbow. One slightly larger than the others. There I stood, just watching them ooze red that trickled away from the wounds and suddenly a wave of calm washed over me. The tears had stopped. The anger and hatred had stopped. Now there was nothing. Just nothing.

# Chapter 15

A warm summer's day, the sun beating down on my arm as I was driving to the local supermarket. Black cardigan sleeves attracting the heat but covering the shame. My phone ringing beside me as I waited for the town bridge to settle itself and the barriers to lift. It was Chris.

"What have you forgotten?" There was always something else he wanted me to get.

"Where abouts are you?"

"Stuck at the bridge. Why?"

"There's two police officers here. They need to speak with you."

"Is it about the investigation?"

"No. You really need to come home."

My heart leapt into my throat. I thought I was going to throw up. This had to be serious. Maybe someone had been in an accident. My children? My parents? One of my brothers? Oh God! Oh God! My mind racing with horrendous images and scenarios but nothing like what I was about to be told.

I walked in to find a tubby, middle aged, gentleman in a striped shirt and a slender young woman in a floaty summer dress sitting at my dining table. Both sporting lanyards with official ID cards. He stood slightly, leaned across the table and introduced himself, shaking my hand and showing his badge. He indicated to the woman on his left and introduced her too. She was part of the police safeguarding and social work team. I was confused.

"Please, sit down Miss Hadley. What we need to discuss with you is a very serious matter that may come as a bit of shock to you."

Oh, Jesus! Have I been reported for something? Am I being investigated? Oh my God! Am I going to be arrested? Shit! Shit! Shit!

Uncontrollable trembling saw me weak in the legs anyway and so I sat across the table from these imposing figures.

"Miss Hadley, is it right that you have recently resided at this address?" He indicated the address on a piece of paper. It was the address where Stuart and my children were currently living. The home I had left.

"Yes. I left about five months ago, following the breakdown of my marriage."

"Are you able to get hold of your ex-husband as we haven't been able to?"

"I'll try to call him now. He'll probably be at his parents. Do you want him to come here?"

"That would be helpful if he could."

I called Stuart and he arrived within minutes.

"The reason I need to have this meeting with you is very serious but I must have your complete discretion and I need you to agree not to discuss anything you are told outside of this meeting."

We all agreed.

"Can you describe your neighbours to me at number twelve."

"Tall, greying, Welsh gentleman," Stuart said, standing in his normal arrogant, arms crossed stance.

"And by what name do you know him?"

"Roy." We said in unison.

"And does anyone else live at that address?"

"Yes. His partner Margaret. I work with her at the college," I said.

"Oh! Right. Well that's news to us. I will need to speak with you about that after, if that's okay?" He continued, "Roy Flood as you know him is actually Leonard Royston Flood and he is a convicted paedophile on the sex offenders register. I am his allocated police officer that keeps a regular check on his capability to live a normal life without acting upon his desires and endangering the public. I met with Leonard this morning and he admitted to me that over the last year he had been grooming you all, as a family, to form an unhealthy relationship with your children."

You couldn't make this shit up!

My head was spinning. Had he just told us we were preyed upon by a sex offender and all this time we thought he was just a kind neighbour. He wanted to do things to my children? He wanted to steal their innocence, violate them, hurt them!

I ran to the bathroom and vomited so hard I thought my eyes would leave their sockets. I cleaned myself up and went back to the dining room. Stuart was pacing like a wildcat. I could see the fire tearing through him. His fists clenched so hard his knuckles were white, but this time his rage was not directed at me.

"Are you fucking kidding me? There's sick fucks like that living that close to a primary school. Prime spot for easy pickings. You're a fucking joke. I'm going to fucking kill him!" My wall took the impact of Stuart's vicious blow.

"Mr. Flood will be moving to a different area today. Well away from you and your family to ensure your safety and he is never to contact any of you again."

"Well, if he's leaving today then I'd better fucking catch hold of him now!" With that Stuart left. We could hear his tyres screeching round street corners for some distance.

The gentleman officer made a quick phone call.

Chris made us all a cup of tea and we sat discussing the issue and what we need to look out for in the children in case anything had already occurred. My stomach turned again and again throughout.

Finally, the officers left and the tears fell again. I'm not sure what was said between Chris and I after that, if anything.

I sat there numb.

The Prosecco came to my aid once more and I'll relieve the pain later.

# Chapter 16

We'd found a new house.

I hated this town now. Hated the grubbiness of the streets, the people, even the air seemed to linger with that tinge of sleazy, scummy wasters draining the welfare state. We needed a fresh start and I had a plan.

I kept this plan to myself and we shifted all our belongings from our pokey two-bedroom house to our new, almost palatial, four-bedroom home. Our furniture looked pretty ridiculous in the enormous high-ceilinged rooms. Original wooden beams and large windows of the converted workhouse had enchanted us from the moment we stepped through the door on the first viewing. The countryside views were amazing and there was so much space for the children to play, inside and out.

The court process was dragging as Stuart was unable to pay solicitor fees. He'd been under the impression he would be entitled to a paid solicitor but now it seems that's not the case. I'm not too up to date with the benefits system but why should he get it for free? He should get a bloody job.

The first paperwork to be sent to all parties was a copy of my statement. Of course, the shit hit the fan with Maxine and Chris. Obviously, she didn't like what was being brought to court and took photographs of the sections that she took offence to, sending them as attachments with abusive messages. This was to be her ultimate wrong move. You see the document clearly states on the front that it's only for the parties involved in the case which are clearly listed on the front page. Stuart and I. It also clearly states that it is a legal document. Maxine taking photographs of a copy of my legal documentation and then being able to show it to anyone or even post it on social media, never mind using it against Chris, was severely breaking the conditions of her harassment warning. So, I spent the afternoon on the phone to a lovely police officer who assured me that it would be dealt with accordingly.

To be honest, I'd had a gut full of all this crap and just wanted a quiet life. Maxine's second harassment warning was issued and, basically, she couldn't even say my name it had so many restrictions. This time, however, if she was to break any of them then she would be arrested and charged.

We began to relax and the kids were loving the new house. They made new friends with the local children and they would disappear off up the fields to play all day and only come home for food. That's what a childhood should be like. Full of imagination and adventure.

The Easter holiday came around quickly and Cadence and Alex were loving being here. Talking of not wanting to live with daddy and fretting about how many days they had left before they had to leave. On one occasion, I was taking them both to the shop with me and Alex burst in to tears when I asked him to put his shoes on.

"Oh, sweetheart," a comforting hug, "whatever is the matter?"

"I don't want to go to Daddy's!"

"We're not going to Daddy's, darling. We're only going to the shops for some food bits. You soppy thing. Come on, let's get your shoes on and when we get there you can drive the trolley. How about that?"

The huge grin and cute giggle of relief and he was back to my boisterous, bouncy little boy. God, I love them so much.

The evening was warm as the sunset behind the trees out of the kitchen window. The children were speaking to their father on the phone telling him of pirate adventures and building a den. The volume was loud enough for me to hear his responses and he barely seemed interested. Near the end of the conversation he asked Cadence to pass the phone to me as he had something he needed to ask. She did so and sat next to me at the dining table.

"What the fuck are you playing at?" What a polite greeting.

"I'm sorry?" I was completely baffled.

"Don't fucking play dumb with me, bitch! You're petitioning for divorce as well as custody of the kids and you're saying I was abusive! What the fuck?!"

"Erm, I don't know if you can hear yourself but I can tell you now that the volume is loud enough on this phone for Cadence to hear you as she is sat right next to me, so, do you want to tone it down a bit with the language, Stuart?"

"No, I fucking don't! You want to know what being abusive is really like? Well, do ya? I'll fucking show you the next time I see ya? We'd all be better off if you were fucking dead anyway. I told Cadence the other day that I should have killed you and that she and Alex would be better off with my parents because I would be doing time for murder!"

"Oh, did you now?! Well that just reinforces my case and when CAFCASS, the children and family court advisory and support service, talk with the children I hope she tells them that."

This wasn't how I wanted my plan to be executed but I'd bided my time long enough and there was no way I was letting my children go back to such a vile human being.

"I tell you what, Stuart, get on to your solicitor again tomorrow because the children aren't coming home. They're staying here with me. Where they should be!" I hung up and turned my phone off.

Cadence climbed into my arms in tears and said, "Is that true, Mummy? We can stay here with you?"

"Yes, sweetheart. I'm never letting you two go again."

# Chapter 17

The children loved their new home and new schools. They had settled quickly and made some great new friends and so had I. Many of the local businesses had their children at the same school and they were very intelligent, hardworking, wealthy people. Such a contrast to the conversations I was having a couple of months back.

Maxine had tried her damnedest to cause yet more trouble the evening that I'd told Stuart I was keeping the children. We had a knock at the door at about ten thirty p.m. and two uniformed police officers were stood there. I told them we'd been expecting them and invited them in. We sat at the table and explained the whole situation. They were shocked at the amount of stress we had been through of late and how we seemed to be holding it together so well. (Outwardly you're doing great, Bex, but inwardly we know otherwise. Still hiding a few scars.) They went on to say that they had been sent to check on Chris's children as Maxine was concerned about their welfare. First time for everything I suppose!

The officers had to have a walk round and check that the children were okay. They were all tucked up, sound asleep. The officers were very interested in the house and its history and we had quite a light-hearted conversation with them amid complaints that they had to climb three sets of stairs. It was all in jest though and they were more than satisfied that the children were safe and well. Before leaving, the more senior officer advised me to contact the local police station in the morning and make an appointment to speak with someone. This would have to be logged as an incident against Maxine's harassment warning. He also said that they would be paying a visit to Maxine and caution her about wasting police time. They left, wishing us a pleasant evening.

Today, though, was the court hearing and I was sick to my stomach. I'd smartened up with a new dress with three quarter length sleeves, covering any opportunity of anyone finding out about the self-harming. A small heel, little make-up and tied back hair giving me the sophisticated, reliable, professional look I was trying to achieve. Chris came with me. He had been my rock. He was so sure that this was going to go in my favour but I still had that niggling feeling.

Sitting in a dull waiting room with four small offices to one side was not how I imagined it at all. My solicitor had informed me that she would be unavailable to represent me that day and so, had arranged for someone she knew to replace her. It turned out to be one of the highest respected barristers in the area and she reminded me of my aunt. She was welcoming, yet had a harshness to her tone. She was very matter-of-fact and no nonsense. I had no doubt that she would be very efficient in getting the job done.

I never knew that most of the work when in court was done outside of the courtroom. My representative and Stuart's representative were to-ing and fro-ing for about two hours with negotiations and requests. Stuart had backed down and agreed to have a shared custody agreement and he would have the children every weekend.

Well, if that's all agreed, why are we here?

Nerves were starting to get the better of me when we were eventually called through. The clerk had told us what we needed to do regarding how to address the judges and so on.

The room was quite sizeable but, definitely, an after-thought. I had been to a magistrate court before on many occasions when on a school trip with some of my students. They had been wooden benched and cleanly decorated with the crossed swords proudly presented. This room, however, was probably an old store room that was in the process of being converted. The walls were an off-white wood-chip wallpaper with a cluster of what looked like school desks arranged to one side of the room. I couldn't quite make out what or how the dock area was constructed as the Perspex was reflective, I guess so as not to be able to see someone's face.

Stuart sat closest to the judges as the prosecution and I sat directly opposite the judges as a defendant. My hands clasped together, sweaty in my lap. My legs trembling. I sat straight and prayed that it wasn't obvious how utterly petrified I was. I think the only thing that I had to say was my name for the tape before the session commenced. My barrister was great and very to the point. The judges saw it unreasonable to put the children through the upheaval of changing schools once more and was complimentary on the maturity that we had both shown in putting the best interests of the children before anything else.

I left the room with the biggest smile on my face. Chris was delighted. A firm hand shake for each of us from my representative and she was off to her next case. I could see out of the corner of my eye that Stuart was surrounded by the family members he had brought with him and decided it best not to hang around. Chris and I headed for the exit as quickly as we could and home to celebrate.

I don't remember how many phone calls I made when I got home or how many glasses of wine I had, but that was under better control these days and nowhere near as much as I had previously been drinking. The children had joined in the celebrations, eating sweets and dancing crazily with us in the front room to cheesy pop classics. Life was now as it should be and we can work on moving forward.

I hadn't noticed the flashing red light of the phone message indicator before but there it was and I hit the play button.

"Hello, this is Doctor Raylon with a message for Rebecca Hadley. Could you please call me at the surgery as a matter of urgency!"